CONTENTS

The Adventures of Obama the Doge

INTRODUCTION

There once was a tail...I mean tale, that devoured this land with fear. What people didn't know was that this tale was the start of a new dimension. This story was about a dog but people called him, a doge. His name was Obama. Obama the Doge. He was the president of the upside-down America and this tale was about him and his strange ways of life. But there was one thing that nobody knew about this dog...he was getting fat on cheese. Oh yeah, he was also green.

CHAPTER 1: SPACE

One day, Obama was just sat there, you know, just doing the general president stuff. All of a sudden…he got a knock on his door. It was a figure dressed in all black. He called himself Mr. Man because he was male. Mr. Man warned Obama that somebody might be after him. Obama said, "Bobar," which was his usual greeting. He then said, "You must be saying nonsense to try to trick me. I'm pretty sure you shouldn't be knocking on the door of the Black House, now get out!" The Black House was upside-down America's equivalent to the White House. Before leaving, Mr. Man responded, "I'm just part of the government and I am advising that you should be more cautious with what you do." Obama slammed the door shut. Time to eat some cheese, thought Obama. He liked all cheese but Camembert, which made him fat, was his favourite. Suddenly, he got another knock at the door, much louder this time. It was a man with an anonymous mask on his face. This man grabbed Obama by the paws and started yanking Obama towards him. He eventually chucked him down onto the hard ground which made Obama become unconscious.

Once he eventually woke up, he was fine but his head had a bit less green fur on it. It came off with the blow. He was trapped in a World War I trench; the only place he could go was to the toilet. Although it was a trench, he could not see any light, it was all dark; he was barely able to see his own paws. He knew trenches well, even in the dark, as he knew his history. Since he was good at history, he knew how to escape the trenches. He used his tail like a lasso to yank himself up. Next, Obama discovered he was not on Htrae anymore (Earth in this upside-down dimension), he was on...Mars (bet you thought this would've been called Sram in this dimension, but no, this dimension makes no sense). At least, he guessed it was Mars as everything was red and stuff. Obama met the anonymous mask holder again and he asked this man a question.

"What did you do with me and why did you do it?" quizzed Obama. The man responded, "I am doing testing on you. We know what you really are." (You'll find out what he really is later on in the book).

Obama started to have a panic attack. Don't worry too much, in a dog's world, a panic attack just means he marches on the spot. After his brief panic attack, Obama said (in his best Mr. Bean voice), "I'll just go sit in the corner and look at some paintings." The anonymous man responded, "If you're not going to be sensible then, drumroll please... I will take you back to where you came from." He then lifted his mask and, probably not surprisingly, he was an alien. The alien threw a banana skin onto Obama's head and slid it down, all the way, to his tail. Obama then started chasing his tail but the alien had actually replaced it with a banana. "Ew, ew, ew!" screamed Obama when he bit into the banana which was actually his own tail. All this talk of bananas has made me want a banana smoothie, BRB.

Ahh, I got my smoothie, now back to the

story.

So, Obama takes away the mask because he was very smart and he knew that if he took away the mask, he would take away the alien's power. So, yeah. Obama 1, Alien 0. But there was one problem – he could not get home. Eventually, he figured out that if he eventually wore the mask, he would eventually be able to figure out that eventually he could fly back home... eventually. "Bobar!" Obama said to Mars ("Bobar" was how he said his farewells). He was now safe and sound in the Black House. He put the mask away on the shelf in one of the secret cabinets and locked it away, said, "Bobar" and went away to do his president things. That's the end of chapter 1.

CHAPTER 2: POO

If you are a dog, a fly or a dung beetle, this is the chapter for you.

Obama the Doge was just strolling away from troubles and eventually, he came across a poo on the floor. Obama said to himself, "That's probably the work of these humans – I'm going to call them poomans from now on." He threw his half-eaten packet of cheese and onion Hula-Hoops into the sun for no general reason. Obama started walking around the poo; sniffing around it. He did this for hours. After a long while, Obama stopped and wondered why he liked sniffing poo so much. Who knows? I know. I'm the author. I can imagine this being used in a school one day, discussing predictions as to why Obama liked sniffing poo.

Tragedy struck - Obama died because of how stinky the poo was. But Obama, tragically, revived himself from the dead. Then he wandered over to the city again, bringing the poo with him inside a rubber ducky. Next, something cool happened. The poo fell on Obama's head and then something really good happened. He ate it.

BRB, I've just got to go puke in the toilet.

Some terrible news, by the way, Obama is heading off to Paradise City. Oh no, that's just the song I'm listening to. He was actually going to Dump Truck Island, which was a festival in the name of all dogs and presidents. So, basically, just Obama. Once he got to the festival, he eventually made a massive fool of himself because his phone sent a notification when he was doing a big, grand speech. It was a voicemail which played out loud and automatically, "YOUR TEST HAS COME BACK POSITIVE FOR EXPLOSIVE DIARRHOEA!" The audience burst out laughing. "Hahahahaha!" Obama launched a nuke on their heads. Obama was then stuck in Russia, for some reason. Eventually, the poo that he ate came out the other end but it was all runny and sticky, he did feel it. What did he do with his runny and sticky poo? He obviously ate it. He loved eating poo almost as much as he loved eating cheese. After a while, he puked but he didn't eat his puke. What he did do with it though, is put it on his bum, then his bum sucked it all up. Then it came out of his mouth, once again (reverse eating).

You should write this down. Oh no, sorry I was just talking to my assistant. He's called Dave.

Next, Obama did a massive poo which covered the whole Htrae (Earth spelled backwards, remember). It began to mix with the atmosphere which eventually made a lot of people, but not all the people, into zombie poo monsters who were out to get Obama for what he had done. He phoned Mr. Man, from the previous chapter, and Mr. Man said, "Told you so." and just hung up. Obama decided to phone Mrs. Woman. She was called Mrs. Woman because she was female. Mrs. Woman was not a zombie poo monster but she was a zombie wee monster which was very bad but the wee monsters weren't out to get Obama. They were out to get Biden who was a business owner and future president. Mrs. Woman only offered to help if Obama offered to help destroy Biden. Obama agreed but he didn't really mean it as he and Biden were friends. Mrs. Woman helped to kill and destroy all the zombie poo monsters (just kidding, she turned them back to people; I'm not a monster). She, luckily, had a secret wee gun and when she used it, the poo got safely flushed down the toilet and no clogs were left. Once Mrs. Woman figured out that Obama was not going to help her in return, she got into a minor rage which led to a wee zombie apocalypse. Does Obama survive that apocalypse? You'll find out in the next chapter.

CHAPTER 3: MEETING HIS TWIN

15 years after the wee zombie apocalypse broke out, Obama was still alive which was pretty good for a doge. There were only three other people alive. These people were:

1. Obama
2. Obama's assistant and friend. He was called Derek.
3. Obama's Vice President. She was called Grace.
4. Joe Biden

These people teamed up and created T.S.O.W or The Survivors of Wee. They were hiding out in a bunker in the middle of the desert. It was a traditional desert with sand and cacti. But, suddenly, a wee zombie broke in. It was just a kid zombie but... it had parents! They broke in as well. T.S.O.W magically disappeared. Nobody knew why but they were teleported to the grand, the great, the magical, zombie-free land they once lived in. Everyone had returned from the dead and nobody knew what happened. You may find out more at the end of this chapter but I don't know, I don't get told anything.

All of a sudden, Obama checked his calendar. It was time for his twin to visit. So, he put on a huge, grand welcoming party in the Black House and invited loads of guests. As soon as his twin showed his massive face, Obama said nervously, "Here he is..." then, "Bobar." The crowd all went, "Well, where is he?" Obama replied, "There. That fly. By the way, I'm a fly too. I would like one volunteer to lift off my head." A guy called Mike did it. Somehow, this tiny creature was controlling this massive, green doge. Now everyone had found out that Obama was actually a fly. Obama then sat down to watch some TV. As he switched to the news channel, he saw a lady talking about him.

"Some shocking news. Our loyal president, Obama the Doge, turns out to have been a fly this whole time. Experts think that this might have been why he had a test for explosive

diarrhoea and it may also be the reason why he swallowed his own poo in chapter 2. Thank you and over to you Bob."

After hearing about himself on the news, he thought to himself, 'Should I give away my second secret? Nah. They'll find out eventually anyway.' He suddenly remembered he had to go and collect his dog head from Mike. So, he went and retrieved the head to only find out, he was already wearing it! Mike had put it straight back on after the shock of finding out Obama was a fly.

Why do we think Obama likes sniffing poo? Because he's a fly, teach. Did anyone predict this?

Suddenly, Obama got stuck in a dance spell for no intelligent reason. Kids always love that. When Obama felt like fainting because of how tired he was, some people broke into the dance room. Because he was in a dance room for some reason, full of music and no people. And then, suddenly, he realised it was Mr. Man and Mrs Woman. Suddenly, clones of Mr. Man and Mrs. Woman came in but they were the old versions of them (the wee zombie and the poo zombie!) but they friendly. Phew! Then, and I'm not going to use suddenly again, the clones' heads exploded and then marshmallows came out which in this world meant that somebody was controlling them and something had malfunctioned. That's the end of chapter 3.

CHAPTER 4: THE GREAT ESCAPE

Well, stuff happened and eventually Obama got out and everything was back to normal. He tried to name all the states but could only think of three. He decided to do something else.

Obama went out litter picking. The two strangest things he came across was a baby's bottle and a pair of socks. He actually found the pair of socks on the street, not even a field. "Bobar!" said Obama as he tapped a stranger on the head. This stranger actually turned out to be a time traveller. All of a sudden, they both teleported to two thousand billion years into the future and all of a sudden, Obama felt the big bang. They were still on Htrae but something terrible had happened. The time traveller had noticed Obama the Doge but he didn't make a big mess of it. The Time Traveller said to Obama, "This is not the big bang you have heard of. This is the big boil. All the water on Htrae boiled until the whole planet exploded." (They were currently floating in space where Htrae once was). After the Time Traveller showed him that, Obama started licking stuff. Mostly rocks and the Time Traveller. The truth is, no one ever really knew why the Time Traveller brought Obama to this time. Yes, yes, yes. Yes, that is right. I'm pretty sure.

Oh, my goodness, little Johnny has just come in. He's the world's smartest predictor. Prediction time. What do we think will happen next? *'I think that a drawer will open and a marshmallow will pop out,'* said Ruben. Great prediction. I really love it. Little Johnny said, *'There was alien in this time, from Jupiter, and it took Obama to his home planet.'* Be quiet, little Johnny. You're talking nonsense and no one likes you. Embarrassing. No, wait, that was actually it. Very good little Johnny.

So, Obama had been taken through space, to Jupiter, by an alien. Things happened during the 92 weeks he was there and, yeah, he met another dog who was being held hostage. He was from a far away galaxy called the Milky Way; the planet he was from was called Earth. His name was Barney. Last name, Bradford. Barney Bradford. So, yeah. One day, the guys just decided to escape. Once they had escaped, they flew back to Htrae only to find, without their president, everything was war. So, yeah, but Barney was super special. He had the power of world peace. He just stopped it, like that. Bang.

It wasn't really a great escape, like the title suggested.

CHAPTER 5: GETTING FAT ON CHEESE

Barney and Obama decided that it was time to have a rest so Obama went back to the Black House with Barney. Obama gave him a grand tour and showed Barney his cheese collection: Camembert, Swiss and so many others (I can't be bothered to name them all). Obama started eating like mad. He said it was a habit. Once he starts eating, he can't control himself. "I'm afraid that something tragic is about to happen," said a deep voice, coming from the cheese. It was a bacterium on the cheese, called Mike. Obama said, "Bobar, Mike. Do you know you are on my cheese? You'd better get off my cheese before I squish you." So, the little bacterium called Mike ate lima beans all over Obama's cheese which was very weird because Obama didn't want his cheese tasting like lima beans but he did squish Mike, which was the good part. Then, all of a sudden, Obama started eating again, like mad. Barney was just watching all this tragic stuff. The ground started shaking as Barney was hungry because he was a dog, like Obama, and watching another dog eat was terrible, so yeah. Obama didn't share his food so Barney took it, but then Obama ate Barney but, all of a sudden, from inside his tum-tum, he felt some tummy ache and he got swallowed by Barney from the inside out. This repeated for around 50 hours until Obama was getting too fat to deal with it. Barney wasn't fat at all though, as that isn't how it works it his world. Obama split his dog costume and was now only left with his fly one because he wasn't actually a fly! Isn't that exciting reader? Isn't it? Isn't it!?!

Obama travelled one metre to meet his friend Barney and once they had met, they all travelled to a place to go on holiday. A place around 4 inches away from them: the box of cheese. They all had so much cheese; Obama's fly costume was starting to rip. He said he should stop eating cheese right now as he did not want to reveal what he actually was. Although, he did really want to come clean because he wanted people to trust him and not just think he has many secrets (which he does. So, yeah). A window flew over to Barney and teleported him home.

Obama had to go to a festival. It was Dump Truck Island (again). This time it was for his grand army testing; to say who was going into the army, but they didn't call it an army here - they called it a leggy. So, as he was on his way there, Obama started to notice that people did not look as happy as they used to. For some reason, Obama rolled down his window and asked them why they looked sad. They responded by telling him that it is because he is a fly and they only respected doges and humans and they didn't like their country anymore. He said, "Well, good gracious!" in his best British accent, "Well good gracious me and GET OUT OF MY WAY!" Obama was sad now because they didn't accept him for who he was not.

After he arrived on stage, Obama said to his subjects, "These are the leggy people who are going to be joining..." He introduced quite a few people who were joining the leggy. Stuff then happened that was too violent to describe. After the violent events, Mr. Cheese entered. He was called Mr. Cheese because he was cheese. Obama didn't like this person as he was made out of cheese but he couldn't eat him. Mr. Cheese did stuff and eventually managed to make Obama eat more cheese which was a *bad* thing. He split his fly costume. He was a monster. He was not from the world of Htrae. He was not even from this town. He was from Jupiter (not Retipuj, as you may have thought). The crowd were shocked. "Oh, my goodness!" "Oh, mio Dio!" (Someone in the audience was Italian). The crowd then booed and threw nothing at Obama.

Eventuuuuuuuuuuuuuaaaaaaaaaaaaaaaalllll lllllllyyyyyy, Obama pooed. The reason he was a green doge was because he had not studied Htrae enough to know that dogs weren't usually green.

Quick game of 'Would you Rather': would you rather poo on Obama or wee on Obama?

Answer: Neither.

Obama went on a rampage, destroying nothing and eating cheese. After Obama was done rampaging around like a maniac, he said, "Sorry," and they all lived happily ever after. Bobar.

THE END.

ABOUT THE AUTHOR

Ruben Brook

Ruben Brook is a 9 year old home schooler from North Lincolnshire, UK. Diagnosed as neuro-diverse, Ruben started his home schooling journey as a way to approach his learning in a more practical and engaging way.

His achievements to date have included the creation of a YouTube channel, a small business that sells fidget toys and now creating an e-book!

A huge thank you to DV for helping out with this story!